WAKEY WAKEY BIG BROWN BEAR!

WRITTEN BY
TRACEY CORDEROY

ILLUSTRATED BY
RACHEL SWIRLES

For Mum x
R.S.

For Bramble,
with my love always x
T.C.

First published in 2012
by Meadowside Children's Books
185 Fleet Street, London, EC4A 2HS
www.meadowsidebooks.com

Text © Tracey Corderoy 2012
Illustrations © Rachel Swirles 2012
The rights of Tracey Corderoy and Rachel Swirles
to be identified as the author and illustrator
of this work has been asserted by them in accordance
with the Copyright, Designs and Patents Act, 1988

A CIP catalogue record for this book
is available from the British Library
1 2 3 4 5 6 7 8 9 10
Printed in China

meadowside

Autumn was coming. Bright berries shone
like jewels, leaves danced to the ground, and it was
time for Big Brown Bear's long sleep. He would sleep
through the pretty Autumn and the sparkly Winter too.
And he wouldn't wake again until the Spring...

SHHH!
(BEAR SLEEPING)

"I'll miss all the fun!"
he yawned.

Little Grey Mouse and Snow Hare tucked
Big Brown Bear into bed and Squirrel
read him a story. Then it was
time for him to sleep.

"You'll be awake
before you know it!"
they said.

BEDTIME STORIES

"But I really want to stay up," sighed Big Brown Bear.

"You see, I've never
rolled in crunchy leaves,

or jumped in
giant rain puddles,

or made a fluffy snow-bear,
just like me!"

"I'll wake you up!" squeaked Little Grey Mouse,
"when the forest is a carpet of leaves.
Then we'll roll in them together, you and me!"

"And we'll jump
in puddles,"
Snow Hare said,

"when the rain
comes tumbling
down!"

"And we'll build a snow-bear together," smiled Squirrel.
"We'll wake you up, you'll see!"

"Thanks," said Big Brown Bear,
his head growing heavy with dreams.

And in a blink, he was fast asleep,
as the wind swept by.

Little Grey Mouse tried to wake his friend
when the forest was a carpet of leaves.

"Wakey Wakey,
Big Brown Bear!"
he called...

but Big Brown Bear
slept on.

"Oh well," sighed Little Grey Mouse.
"I'll keep some crunchy leaves, just in case..."

Snow Hare tried to wake her friend when
the rain came tumbling down.

"Wakey Wakey, Big Brown Bear!"

she called...

but Big Brown Bear
slept on.

"Oooh!" cried Snow Hare.
"Giant puddles!"
And she collected some
raindrops in buckets and bowls,
just in case...

Finally, Squirrel tried to wake his friend
when snowflakes filled the sky.

"Wakey Wakey,
Big Brown Bear!"

he called...

but Big Brown Bear
slept on.

"Wheee!" giggled Squirrel, shaking a pillow until feathers danced down like snowflakes.

"I'll keep a nice big bundle of these, just in case..."

Big Brown Bear was missing all the fun.
"What shall we *do*?" asked Little Grey Mouse.

"We must wait until Spring,"
Snow Hare sighed.

"And *then*," giggled Squirrel,
"I know what we'll do!"
And he whispered a plan to the others...

At last, Big Brown Bear yawned awake. The grass
was soft and green, and bright new leaves filled the trees.
"Oh dear," he sighed. "It must be Spring
and I've missed all the fun."

He rubbed his eyes.

But wait – what was this?

"**Surprise!**" cried all his friends.
"We saved Autumn and Winter
just for you!"

There were crunchy
leaves to roll in,

giant rain puddles
to jump in...

and feathers to build a fluffy
snow-bear too!

"Thank you, thank you!"
cried Big Brown Bear.

But suddenly his friends
had great big yawns. So...

Big Brown Bear tucked them all into bed.
"Night night," he whispered softly, as their heads grew heavy with dreams.
"Night night, Big Brown Bear," they whispered back.